THIS BLOOMSBURY BOOK

BELONGS TO

....

For Michael with all my love

Bloomsbury Publishing, London, Berlin and New York

First published in Great Britain in October 2009 by Bloomsbury Publishing Plc
36 Soho Square, London, W1D 3QY

This paperback edition first published in 2010

Text & illustrations copyright © Debi Gliori 2009
The moral right of the author/illustrator has been asserted

A CIP catalogue record of this book is available from the British Library

ISBN 978 0 7475 9972 2

Printed in Belgium by Proost, Turnhout

1 3 5 7 9 10 8 6 4 2

FSC
Mixed Sources
Product group from well-managed
forests and recycled wood or fibre
Cert no. BV-COC-070303
www.fsc.org
© 1996 Forest Stewardship Council

This book is printed with vegetable inks

www.bloomsbury.com/childrens

Stormy Weather

Debi Gliori

BLOOMSBURY

LONDON BERLIN NEW YORK

Pull up the quilt, turn out the light,
dear child, it's time to say goodnight.
In darkness black and soft and deep,
I'll watch beside you while you sleep.

Across the world
in many beds
a million goodnight
stories read

of frogs and kings
and gingerbread,
then lights go out,
goodnights are said.

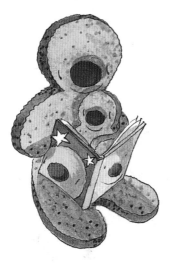

Then should the oceans roar and rise
and dark clouds race
across the skies

I'd hold you tight and close and warm
and keep you safe all through the storm.

If thunder tore the night in two
and lightning played at peek~a~BOO

we'd watch the storm pass overhead,
then curl up safe and snug in bed.

And if that breeze became a gale ~
whipped leaves, snapped twigs, made branches flail

I'd wrap you safely in my wings
and tell you tales of sleepy things.

And if it rained ten thousand rains
and torrents swept down streets to drains

we'd build a boat and sail away
to where the sun shines bright all day.

And if the snow began to fall,

flake on flake piled up miles tall

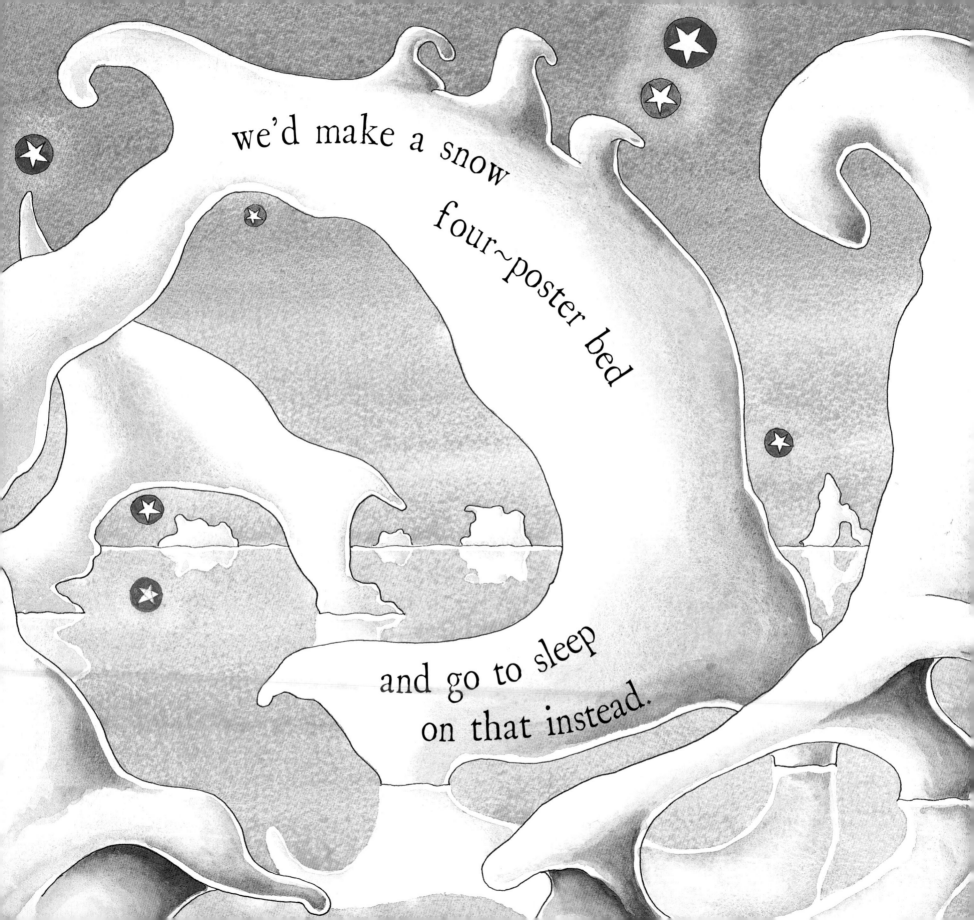

we'd make a snow
four~poster bed

and go to sleep
on that instead.

From North to South and East to West,
from cave to berg and twig to nest
a sleepy hush across the world,
small creatures in their beds are curled.

Sweet dreams beneath our sheltering sky,
the tides and winds our lullaby,

the stars our light, the whole night through
shine down so bright on me and you.

More magical moments to share,
from Debi Gliori . . .

'A brilliant gem of a book'
Guardian

'Gliori's quirky pictures and
couplets are full of humour, as well as
an important message'
The Times